HELEN BANNERMAN

THE STORY

of

LITTLE BABAJI

*illustrated
by*

FRED MARCELLINO

HarperCollins Publishers

THE STORY *of* LITTLE BABAJI

Once upon a time there was a little boy, and his name was Little Babaji.

And his Mother was called Mamaji.

And his Father was called Papaji.

And Mamaji made him a beautiful little Red Coat, and a pair of beautiful little Blue Trousers.

And Papaji went to the Bazaar, and bought him a beautiful Green Umbrella, and a lovely little Pair of Purple Shoes with Crimson Soles and Crimson Linings.

And then wasn't Little Babaji grand?

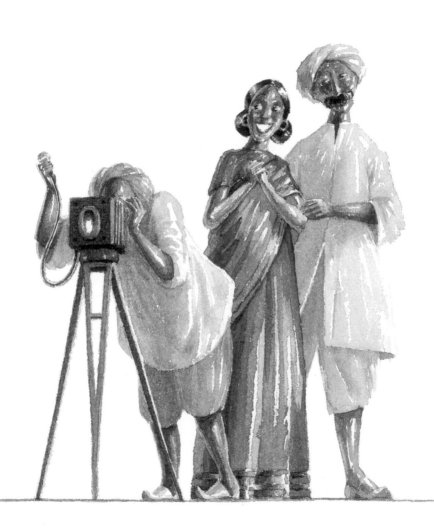

So he put on all his Fine Clothes, and went out for a walk in the Jungle.

And by and by he met a Tiger. And the Tiger said to him, "Little Babaji, I'm going to eat you up!"

And Little Babaji said, "Oh! Please Mr. Tiger, don't eat me up, and I'll give you my beautiful little Red Coat." So the Tiger said, "Very well, I won't eat you this time, but you must give me your beautiful little Red Coat."

So the Tiger got poor Little Babaji's beautiful little Red Coat, and went away saying, "Now I'm the grandest Tiger in the Jungle."

And Little Babaji went on, and by and by he met another Tiger, and it said to him, "Little Babaji, I'm going to eat you up!" And Little Babaji said, "Oh! Please Mr. Tiger, don't eat me up, and I'll give you my beautiful little Blue Trousers." So the Tiger said, "Very well, I won't eat you this time, but you must give me your beautiful little Blue Trousers."

So the Tiger got poor Little Babaji's beautiful little Blue Trousers, and went away saying, "Now *I'm* the grandest Tiger in the Jungle."

And Little Babaji went on and by and by he met another Tiger, and it said to him, "Little Babaji, I'm going to eat you up!" And Little Babaji said, "Oh! Please Mr. Tiger, don't eat me up, and I'll give you my beautiful little Purple Shoes with Crimson Soles and Crimson Linings."

But the Tiger said, "What use would your shoes be to me? I've got four feet, and you've got only two. You haven't got enough shoes for me."

But Little Babaji said, "You could wear them on your ears."

"So I could," said the Tiger, "that's a very good idea. Give them to me, and I won't eat you this time."

So the Tiger got poor Little Babaji's beautiful little Purple Shoes with Crimson Soles and Crimson Linings, and went away saying, "Now *I'm* the grandest Tiger in the Jungle."

And by and by Little Babaji met another Tiger, and it said to him, "Little Babaji, I'm going to eat you up!" And Little Babaji said, "Oh! Please Mr. Tiger, don't eat me up, and I'll give you my beautiful Green Umbrella." But the Tiger said, "How can I carry an umbrella, when I need all my paws for walking with?"

"You could tie a knot on your tail and carry it that way," said Little Babaji. "So I could," said the Tiger. "Give it to me, and I won't eat you this time."

So he got poor Little Babaji's beautiful
Green Umbrella, and went away saying,
"Now *I'm* the grandest Tiger in the Jungle."

And poor Little Babaji went away crying, because the cruel Tigers had taken all his fine clothes.

Presently he heard a horrible noise that sounded like "Gr-r-r-r-r-rrrrrrr," and it got louder and louder. "Oh! dear!" said Little Babaji, "there are all the Tigers coming back to eat me up! What shall I do?" So he ran quickly to a palm tree, and peeped round it to see what the matter was.

And there he saw all the Tigers fighting, and disputing which of them was the grandest.

And at last they all got so angry that they jumped up and took off all the fine clothes, and began to tear each other with their claws, and bite each other with their great big white teeth.

And they came rolling and tumbling right to the foot of the very tree where Little Babaji was hiding, but he jumped quickly in behind the umbrella. And the Tigers all caught hold of each other's tails, as they wrangled and scrambled, and so they found themselves in a ring round the tree.

Then, when the Tigers were very wee and very far away, Little Babaji jumped up, and called out, "Oh! Tigers! why have you taken off all your nice clothes? Don't you want them any more?" But the Tigers only answered, "Gr-r-rrrrr!"

Then Little Babaji said, "If you want them, say so, or I'll take them away." But the Tigers would not let go of each other's tails, and so they could only say "Gr-r-r-rrrrrr!"

So Little Babaji put on all his fine clothes
again and walked off.

And the Tigers were very, very angry, but still they would not let go of each other's tails.

And they were so angry that they ran round the tree, trying to eat each other up, and they ran faster and faster...

till they were whirling round so fast that you couldn't see their legs at all. And they still ran faster and faster and faster...

till they all just melted away, and there was nothing left but a great big pool of melted butter (or "ghi," as it is called in India) round the foot of the tree.

Now Papaji was just coming home from his work, with a great big brass pot in his arms, and when he saw what was left of all the Tigers he said, "Oh! what lovely melted butter! I'll take that home to Mamaji for her to cook with." So he put it all into the great big brass pot, and took it home to Mamaji to cook with.

When Mamaji saw the melted butter, wasn't she pleased! "Now," said she, "we'll all have pancakes for supper!"

So she got flour and eggs and milk and sugar and butter, and she made a huge big plate of the most lovely pancakes. And she fried them in the melted butter which the Tigers had made, and they were just as yellow and brown as little Tigers.

And then they all sat down to supper.

And Mamaji ate Twenty-seven pancakes,
and Papaji ate Fifty-five.

But Little Babaji ate a Hundred and Sixty-nine, because he was so hungry.

A NOTE ON THE TEXT

Helen Bannerman, who lived in India for thirty years,
wrote and illustrated *The Story of Little Black Sambo* (1899),
a story that clearly takes place in India,
with its tigers and "ghi" (or melted butter).
For this edition of Bannerman's story, the little boy,
his mother, and his father have been given
authentic Indian names.